HOPE is a HOP

written by Katrina Moore illustrated by Melissa Iwai

Dial Books for Young Readers

For Penelope and Benjamin,
my little gardeners and
bunny finders—KM

For my mom, always patient and
nurturing, whose garden overflows with
vegetables and flowers year round—MI

DIAL BOOKS FOR YOUNG READERS
An imprint of Penguin Random House LLC, New York

First published in the United States of America by Dial Books for Young Readers, an imprint of Penguin Random House LLC, 2023

Visit us online at penguinrandomhouse.com.

Library of Congress Cataloging-in-Publication Data is available.
Manufactured in China
ISBN 9780593323854
TOPL

1 3 5 7 9 10 8 6 4 2

Design by Cerise Steel
Text set in Milo Pro

The artwork in this book was created with watercolor, gouache and colored pencil, and collaged digitally in Photoshop.

Hope is a light you turn on in the dark,
an up before sunrise—start of a spark.

Hope is a whisper you say to your heart.

It's a hoe and a hole and a heap in your cart.

Hope is a seed that is too small to spy,
deep in the dirt that's deserted and dry.

Hope is a hum and a song and a pat,

a battle with a bunny . . .

a worn-in straw hat.

Hope is a sprout and a splosh in the mud.

The first pop of pink and a blossoming bud.

When everything's tussled and
turned upside down . . .

EVA'S
GARDEN

When you're thudding and
thumping and covered in brown.

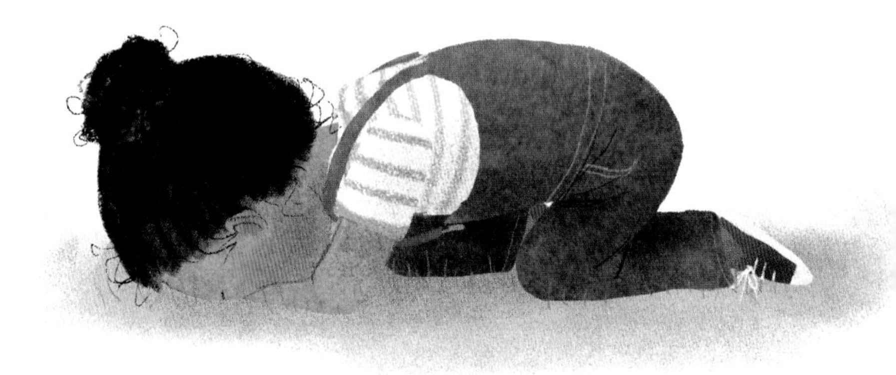

When you're waist high in weeds,
and you're worried you'll drown.

Hope's a soft heartbeat
so loud that it drums.

A new place discovered
from following crumbs.

Hope is eight ears that are huddled as one.

Hope is a hop,

and a skip,

and a run.

It’s new seeds and soil and planting anew.

And waiting

and wishing

for sunshine and dew.

At last, there's a rainbow . . .

all braided
like rope.

New hops . . .

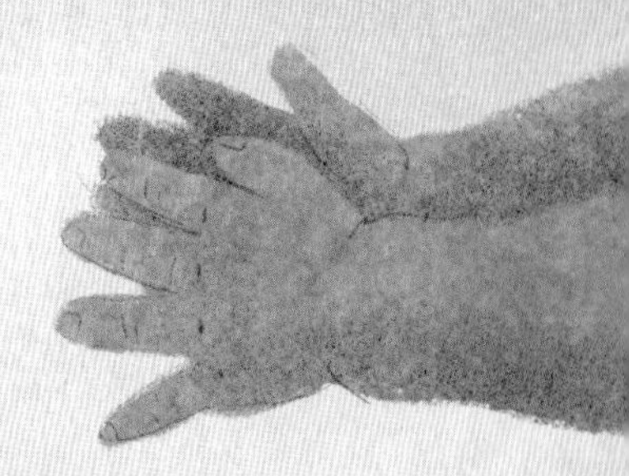

and new hands,

that all sprouted from . . .

HOPE